MORRIS
IN THE
APPLE TREE

Vivian French

Illustrations by Olivia Villet

ROARING GOOD READS

Collins

An imprint of HarperCollins*Publishers*

First published in Great Britain by Collins*Children'sBooks* 1995
This edition published in Great Britain by HarperCollins*Children'sBooks* 2004
HarperCollins*Children'sBooks* is an imprint of HarperCollins*Publishers* Ltd
77-85 Fulham Palace Road, Hammersmith, London W6 8JB

The HarperCollins*Children'sBooks* website address is
www.harpercollinschildrensbooks.co.uk

1 3 5 7 9 8 6 4 2

Text copyright © Vivian French 1995
Illustrations © Olivia Villet 2004

ISBN 0 00 718027 6

The author and illustrator assert the moral right to be
identified as the author and illustrator of the work.

Printed and bound in England by Clays Ltd, St Ives plc

For Clyde, the real Morris
and for Pete – two really cool cats

Chapter One

Morris was ginger and white, and very fat.

He was sitting in the sunshine and
wondering if it was time for dinner.

"I'm sure it must be," he said to
himself. "I'm very hungry."

He went inside to see if dinner was ready.

"GO AWAY," said his mother. "You've only just had breakfast."

"Oh," said Morris. He went back to sit in the sunshine.

Morris cleaned his paws. Then he cleaned his whiskers. Then he cleaned his tummy.

"There," he said to himself. "It must be time for dinner now." He went inside to see.

"GO AWAY," said his big sister Rose. "You've only just had breakfast."

"But I've cleaned my paws," said Morris. "AND my whiskers. AND my tummy. And I'm hungry."

"GO AWAY!" said his mother and Rose together.

Morris went.

Morris walked all the way down to the bottom of the garden.

"It's not fair," he said to himself. "I keep myself all clean and tidy and they won't give me any dinner."

He went to sit under the fence with his back to the house.

"It's just not fair," he said. He closed his eyes and sulked.

"GRRRRRRRRRRRRRR!" There was a
loud and terrible growl, and a large dog
hurled itself at the fence from the other
side.

"MEEEEEOW!" Morris leaped in the air.

"GRRRRRRRRRRRRRR!" The dog jumped up and down. Morris dashed for the nearest tree. He scrambled up it faster than he had ever scrambled anywhere.

Up and up he went, and out along a
branch. At the very end of the branch
he stopped.

"WOOF! Keep off my fence!" said
the dog, and it strolled away.

Rose and her mother heard the dog barking.

"What's going on?" asked Rose.

"Perhaps you'd better go and see," said her mother.

Rose found Morris sitting in the apple tree. His fur was fluffed up all over. It made him look even fatter than usual.

"Whatever are you doing up there?" asked Rose.

"Sitting," said Morris.

"I can see THAT," said Rose, "but WHY? You don't like sitting in trees."

"I know," said Morris. "I was chased."

"CHASED?" Rose stared at him.
Morris nodded.

"Morris," Rose said, "come down here and tell me what happened."

"I can't," said Morris. "I'm stuck."

Chapter Two

"Oh," said Rose. "Are you sure?"

Morris stood up on his branch, and it wobbled.

"MEEEEEOW!" he shrieked, and he held on tightly with all his paws and claws.

"Just jump!" Rose said.

"I can't!" Morris sat down again.
"I'm stuck."

Rose looked at the tree. It looked a
very easy tree to climb.

"Why don't you just turn round and
climb back down?" she asked.

Morris shivered.

"I CAN'T turn round," he said.

Rose sighed. "Oh Morris," she said,
"it's easy! I'll show you!"

She sprang up the tree and stalked
along Morris's branch.

"MEEEEOW!"

Morris hung on grimly as the branch
rocked and swayed.

"Now," said Rose as she sat down beside Morris. "All you have to do is turn round and you'll be back on the ground in no time!"

Morris shook his head.

Rose stood up. "Look, I'll turn right round so you can see how easy it is."

Morris nodded.

There was a pause.

"Well," said Rose, "it SHOULD be easy enough."

There was another pause.

"Morris," said Rose. "I can't turn round."

"No," said Morris.

"Am I stuck?" Rose asked.

"Yes," said Morris.

Chapter Three

Their little brother Tom came bouncing
out of the bushes.

"Hello Morris," he said. "Hello Rose. Why are you sitting in that tree?"

"We're stuck," said Morris. "We can't get down."

"I could get down," said Tom. "If I was stuck in that tree I could just jump down. I'm good at jumping."

"It's a very long way," Morris said.

"No it isn't," said Tom. "Not if you're good at jumping. I'm VERY good at jumping. Look!"

He scrambled up the tree and appeared beside Rose. The branch shook and trembled.

"MEEEEEOW!" said Morris as he
swayed to and fro. "HELP!"

"TOM!" said Rose. "Get down AT
ONCE!"

Tom stood up on the branch. "I'm going to jump," he said. "Watch me jump, Morris. Watch me jump, Rose."

"You be careful," said Rose.

"Scramble down the way you came up."

Morris shut his eyes.

"WATCH ME JUMP!" said Tom.

Morris opened one eye.

Rose held her breath.

Tom suddenly sat down.

"Actually," he said, "I think I'll jump in a little while."

"Tom," said Rose, "turn round and go down NOW!"

Morris opened the other eye. "He can't," he said. "He's stuck too."

Chapter Four

"I'm not," said Tom. He wriggled a little.
"Well, I'm only a little bit stuck."

"Merrrow!" said Morris. "KEEP
STILL!"

The three kittens sat close together on the branch. It was very quiet in the garden.

Morris sighed heavily. "We'll be here for ever and ever," he said.

"Will we really?" asked Tom.

"No," Rose said. "Mother will come and find us very soon."

The three kittens went on sitting.

"Is it very soon yet?" asked Tom.

"I don't think so," said Rose, "but I'm sure it won't be long."

"I'm hungry," said Morris.

"You're always hungry," said Rose.

"Shall we call for Mother?" asked Tom.

"I think she's too far away to hear,"
said Rose.

"She's probably getting our dinner ready," said Morris.

Tom began to cry. "Meeeeow. Meeeeow. MOTHER!"

"WOOF! WOOOF! WOOOOF!"

There was a loud barking from the
other side of the fence below the tree.

Morris and Rose and Tom all
trembled and the branch swayed wildly
to and fro. The three kittens held on
desperately, their paws clutching and
their ears flattened.

"HELP!" Rose shouted.

"MOTHER!" yelled Tom.

"MEEEOW!" howled Morris.

The dog stopped barking and
snuffled through the wooden slats.

"Woof. What are you doing up
there? This is MY fence."

He caught sight of Morris. "WOOOF!
I told YOU to buzz off!"

He began barking again.

"YAH! BOO! I'LL CATCH YOU!
SCAREDY CATS, SITTING IN A TREE,
COME DOWN HERE AND—"

"PSSSSSSSSSSST!" Mother Cat arrived in a flying bundle of claws and teeth and fluffed up fur. She leaped at the fence, and the dog let out a loud howl and disappeared.

"MOTHER!" Morris and Rose and Tom stared down at her with wide open eyes.

"You are brave!" said Rose.

"I want to go home!" said Tom.

"Is dinner ready?" asked Morris.

Chapter Five

Mother Cat sat down and looked up at the tree. Her eyes were narrowed and her tail was twitching.

She did not look at all pleased to see them.

"If there's a way up," she said, "then there's ALWAYS a way down. Tom, turn round and come down here AT ONCE!"

"Yes, Mother," said Tom meekly, and he turned round and scrambled down the tree.

As he arrived on the ground Mother
Cat cuffed him with her paw and sent
him flying back up the path.

"Now you, Rose," said Mother Cat.
Rose stood up. Morris wrapped his
paws round the branch and dug his
claws in. Rose wobbled, and then
ran along the branch and down to
the ground.

"Fancy a great big kitten like you getting stuck!" said Mother Cat.

Rose scampered up the path after Tom.

"Now you, Morris," said Mother Cat.

Morris clung on and shut his eyes.
"I can't," he said.

Mother Cat looked at him. "How did you get up there?" she asked.

"I was chased," said Morris. "And now I'm stuck."

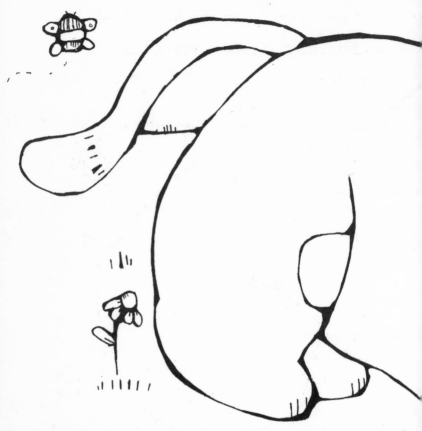

Mother Cat nodded. "Hmmm," she
said. "Well, if you're stuck, you're stuck.
But it's a pity." She stood up and
stretched.

"Your dinner is all ready. It's fresh sardines and your favourite kitty crunchies."

Morris opened his eyes wide.

Mother Cat was rubbing her back against the fence.

"And there's a bowl of cream. Of course, by now Tom and Rose may have eaten it all..."

Morris jumped. He arrived on the ground in a large fluffy heap.

"Goodness me," said Mother Cat.
Morris didn't hear her. He was
hurrying up the path, his tail held high.

The End